Emberley, Rebecca and
Ed Emberley
The Ant and the Grasshopper

JF
EMB

	DATE DUE		
1430	1/31/13		
1/21/16			
4/1/19			

2012

THE ANT AND THE GRASSHOPPER

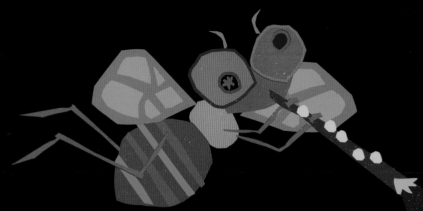

For the people of New Orleans,
with whom we have fallen in love.

Copyright © 2012 by Rebecca Emberley Inc.
A Neal Porter Book
Published by Roaring Brook Press
Roaring Brook Press is a division of Holtzbrinck Publishing Holdings Limited Partnership
175 Fifth Avenue, New York, New York 10010
mackids.com

Library of Congress Cataloging-in-Publication Data

Emberley, Rebecca.
    The ant and the grasshopper / Rebecca Emberley [and] Ed Emberley. — 1st ed.
       p. cm.
    "A Neal Porter book."
    Summary: In this version of the classic fable, a weary ant is energized by the swinging sounds of a grasshopper and his "buggy" band.
    ISBN 978-1-59643 - 493-6 (alk. paper)
[1. Ants—Fiction. 2. Grasshoppers—Fiction. 2. Grasshopper—Fiction. 3. Insects—Fiction. 4. Bands (Music)—Fiction.] I. Emberley, Ed. II. Title.
    P27.E5665An 2012
    [E]—dc23

                                                                                        2011033800

Roaring Brook Press books are available for special promotions and premiums.
For details contact: Director of Special Markets, Holtzbrinck Publishers.

First edition 2012
Book design by Andrew Arnold and Cathy Bobak
Printed in China by Toppan Leefung Printing Ltd., Dongguan City, Guangdong Province

10 9 8 7 6 5 4 3 2 1

THE ANT AND THE GRASSHOPPER

REBECCA EMBERLEY AND ED EMBERLEY

A NEAL PORTER BOOK

Roaring Brook Press • New York

Somewhere on the boulevard of backyards an ant was struggling with the remnants of a picnic.

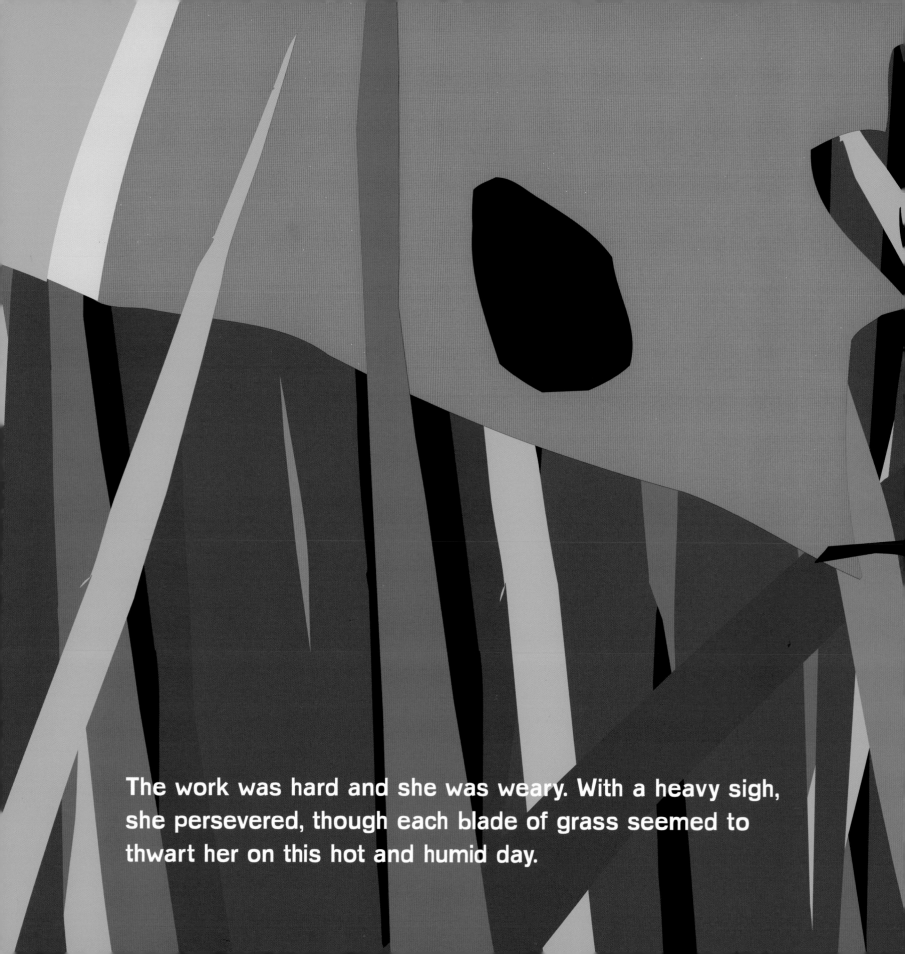

The work was hard and she was weary. With a heavy sigh, she persevered, though each blade of grass seemed to thwart her on this hot and humid day.

"I simply cannot go another step," she thought to herself.

As she lifted her head in hopes of the smallest of breezes to cool her blistering forehead, she heard a sound.

A wonderful, magical sound.

MUSIC.

With a great heave, she shouldered her sticky burden and moved in the direction of the sound.

She came upon a grasshopper and his buggy band
making music with complete abandon.

The ant had never heard such joyful noise. She smiled (which on an ant can look a little strange) and listened to the music, her antennae twitching to the beat.

The weariness seemed to leave her little ant body with every note they played.

When the music stopped the grasshopper called to her, "Hey there, baby, why don't you put down that big sticky thing and come groove with us?"

"I wish I could," said the ant, already feeling a little guilty for stopping for such a long time, "but I must get this back to the colony. My family will be waiting for me." Hoisting her load a little higher she said, "Thank you for your beautiful noise. It has made my heart much lighter."

The band clickety clicked and chirruped, they were so happy to have an audience.

The grasshopper hit an F chord. "We will play for you then, all the way back to your colony." Turning to his bandmates he rasped, "Put on your walking shoes. We're hittin' the road."

The band was all abuzz. The beetle was especially excited as he was the newest member of the band and had never been on the road before.

The ant was home in no time, hardly noticing the heat or the heaviness of her load. "You have made my job so much easier," she said.

"Your magical music moved me along. How can I ever repay you?"

The grasshopper thought for a moment. "Well, baby, our music might be red hot, but we like to be cool. Sometimes it's hard to catch a break out there on the boulevard."

The ant smiled her funky little smile. "It's cool under the ground in our colony. Please come and share your music, and we will have a party!"

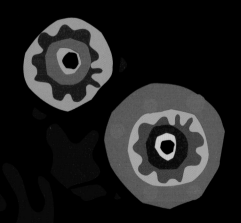

"Come on everybody we're
going underground!"

Let the good times roll!

Laissez les bon temps rouler!

And the music . . .

. . . made everything brighter.